ON THE OTHER SIDE OF THE NIGHT

HOW SCIENCE FICTION AND FANTASY CAN HELP US THROUGH OUR DARK HOUR

STANT LITORE

Westmarch Publishing | 2020

MORE FROM STANT LITORE

COLOSSEUMS FOR DINOSAURS

The Running of the Tyrannosaurs
Nyota's Tyrannosaur
The Screaming of the Tyrannosaur

THE ZOMBIE BIBLE

Death Has Come up into Our Windows
What Our Eyes Have Witnessed
Strangers in the Land
No Lasting Burial
I Will Hold My Death Close
By a Slender Thread (forthcoming)

OTHER TITLES

Ansible: A Thousand Faces
Dante's Heart

The Dark Need (The Dead Man #20)
with Lee Goldberg, William Rabkin

&

Lives of Unforgetting
Lives of Unstoppable Hope
Write Characters Your Readers Won't Forget
Write Worlds Your Readers Won't Forget

ON THE OTHER
SIDE OF THE NIGHT

_____

STANT LITORE

ISBN 978-1-7320869-9-9

You can reach Stant Litore at:
www.stantlitore.com
www.patreon.com/stantlitore

Contents

for everyone who has ever imagined
piloting a spaceship,
riding a dinosaur or a dragon,
or dreamed of a solarpunk city

this book is for you

Chapter One

More Things in Heaven and Earth

A MAN VISITS A MANSION ON THE TOP OF A HILL. HE has not been invited, but he finds the door unlocked. For an instant, he hesitates at the doorstep. His friends in Buenos Aires have told him there is a new resident in the great house in the country, a resident no one has seen, though strange sounds and lights come from the house at night. But it is raining torrents, and that decides him; swiftly, he ducks inside the house.

Once inside, passing from one room to the next, he begins to tremble. Nothing he sees makes sense. There is furniture, but he can't describe it. An armchair implies a human body, but these furnishings imply things he cannot imagine. It is quiet in the house, except for the wild lashing of the rain against the windows. He becomes increasingly certain that the new resident—whom he assumes is out— has not moved here from some other earthly home. The resident is alien.

At last, shaking from revulsion and horror, he enters a last room up a long ramp and discovers inside it something with a recognizable shape: a ladder! He is relieved. Here, at last, is something he understands. He grips the rungs and scampers up, only to find himself entering an upper story whose furnishings are more alien even than those below. Shivering, he wonders:

> What must the inhabitant of this house be like? What must it be seeking here, on this planet, which must have been no less horrible to it than it to us? From what secret regions of astronomy or time, from what ancient and now incalculable twilight, had it reached this South American suburb and this precise night?

JORGE LUIS BORGES

With a start, he realizes suddenly that the rain has stopped; droplets still cling to the window panes, but there is utter silence. Glancing at his watch, he realizes it is 2 a.m., as if he has spent hours exploring and lost in thought, or as if time operates differently inside the house than outside it. He resolves to leave, quickly, before the unseen inhabitant can return. Hardly daring to breathe, he hurries back down the ladder to the rooms below. At that point in the story, Jorge Luis Borges ends his fiction "There Are More Things":

> My feet were just touching the next to last rung when I heard something coming up the ramp—something heavy and slow and plural. Curiosity got the better of fear, and I did not close my eyes.

JORGE LUIS BORGES

This is one of my favorite science fiction stories, because of that final line: *I did not close my eyes.* To me, that is the essence and function of speculative fiction. The best science fiction and fantasy confronts us with characters or apparitions that appear to us to be monsters or marvels and then whispers to us, *Do not close your eyes.* All our lives, so many of us flee from encounters with difference. Speculative fiction invites the encounter, welcomes it, sometimes with a shiver, sometimes with delight, sometimes just with a spirit of wild adventure and the embracing of unforeseen possibilities.

Borges' title, "There Are More Things," is from a line in *Hamlet*, when the Prince of Denmark tells his skeptical friend Horatio, upon encountering a spirit that might be his father's Ghost:

> *There are more things in heaven and Earth, Horatio,*
> *Than are dreamt of in your philosophy.*

HAMLET

What is one to do when one encounters a marvel, when the unexpected invades one's philosophy, one's preconceptions and biases, one's perspective on life and community and the world, coming on unasked, uninvited, like a shock? As the Ghost approaches in its chains, many of the soldiers of Denmark quail and fall back and wish to flee. Hamlet does not. Whether the Ghost will present him with "aught of woe or wonder," he will speak to it. He will face the Ghost. He will not close his eyes.

Woe or wonder: these are two reactions human beings can have to the encounter with the unexpected and the strange. Fear or wonder. In real life, when you run into something or someone who is different from you, someone who speaks differently or believes differently or looks different, or a place or culture or organism you don't fully understand, you have a mix of instinctive responses. You have a mix of wonder and fear. One of those two reactions is going to take priority.

If *fear* takes priority, you are driven to increase the distance between you and what's different from you. There are different ways to seek or enforce such distance. You can pick up an axe and smash the other who frightens you in the head. You can run away. You can freeze in stark terror, like a character in a weird fiction tale confronted by a mass of tentacles and eyeballs slithering near. Or you can take what's different and put it in a cage, confine it and control it so that it stays where you want it while you move about. That's the *fear* response.

But fear is not the *only* response to the strange and unexpected other. The hero of Borges' tale does not close his eyes, does not flee and hide; he faces the being who is coming up the ramp, accepting the encounter and the offer of adventure that it implies. Hamlet rushes out into the dark forest to speak with the Ghost, his wonder and his curiosity overpowering all fear. Aristotle, in his *Metaphysics*, says that wonder is the beginning of all knowledge, all science, all knowing, because wonder provokes us to draw *near* rather than *away*, to give ourselves to the marvelous encounter. To ask questions. You and I, we are *human*. It is ours to wonder at the world and at each other, not to cower and tremble and fear.

Children know this, I think. While they are still small enough, everything seems to them a wonder, something to draw near and touch. It is only by our wounds, by the lick of flame at our fingers or the bite of a wild creature, or the tumble down the scree where we were seeking to pull out a brightly colored rock—it is only by our pain that we learn fear. Fear is not our natural condition. Consider this passage that I read as a youth, in Mary Renault's beautiful novel, *The King Must Die*. In it, young Theseus, as a boy of seven, catches sight of the most magnificent horse:

> Poseidon, as I knew, can look like a man or like a horse, whichever he chooses. In his man shape, it was said, he had begotten me. But there were songs in which he had horse sons too, swift as the north wind, and immortal. The King Horse, who was his own, must surely be one of these. It seemed clear to me, therefore, that we ought to meet. I had heard he was only five years old. "So," I thought, "though he is the bigger, I am the elder. It is for me to speak first."
>
> …Then I saw him, standing by himself on a little knoll, watching the end of the pasture where they were choosing colts. I went nearer, thinking, as every child thinks once for the first time, "Here is beauty."
>
> He had heard me, and turned to look. I held out my hand, as I did in the stables, and called, "Son of Poseidon!" On this he came trotting up to me, just as the stable horses did. I had brought a lump of salt, and held it out to him.
>
> There was some commotion behind me. The groom bawled out, and looking round I saw the Horse Master beating him. My turn would be next, I thought; men were waving at me from the railings, and cursing each other. I felt safer where I was. The King Horse was so near that I could see the lashes of his dark eyes. His forelock fell between them like a white waterfall between shining stones. His teeth were as big as ivory plates upon a war helm; but his lip,

when he licked the salt out of my palm, felt softer than my mother's breast. When the salt was finished, he brushed my cheek with his, and snuffed at my hair. Then he trotted back to his hillock, whisking his long tail. His feet, with which as I learned later he had killed a mountain lion, sounded neat on the meadow, like a dancer's.

MARY RENAULT, *THE KING MUST DIE*

As children, we want to see the King Horse. We want to stand beside him and feel his breath warm on our cheek, feel him lick the salt from our hand, and laugh as he dances over the grass. Fear is not our natural condition. Nor is it unnecessary; the function of fear is to keep us safe. But fear is a survival mechanism, and where our very survival is not at stake, it has no place. Where our survival is not at stake, our response can be *wonder*. That is what we forget when we get a little older than Theseus at the stable. It is a thing that we could *un*forget.

That is what Borges writes into the end of his story; dedicated "to the memory of H. P. Lovecraft," the story also serves as a colleague's gentle rebuke of Lovecraft. Borges seems to say, *Like you, my friend, I, too, can imagine cosmic horrors, strange life that fits no earthly shape. Yet I have enough imagination to consider that our planet would be, at first glance, "no less horrible to it than it to us." I have enough imagination to consider that there might be conversation between minds that appear at first glance incompatible. I imagine that this creature has occupied a human house; I could choose to regard it as cuckoo in the nest or as invader in the homeland, but I could also choose to regard it as a guest, one seeking welcome, one seeking to know us, one setting aside its own fear and horror in order to draw close and look us in the eye. Lovecraft, for all the grandeur and wild beauty of your fiction, your tales of cosmic horror and woe deny their characters and their readers the gift of choice. Faced with difference, you were able to imagine only flight, only fear. I will choose to imagine wonder. Faced with difference, I choose not to close my eyes.*

* * *

Stories give us opportunities to explore our instinctive responses to the other; vicariously, we discover opportunities to either welcome or reject the marvelous encounter with the other. Which we choose is then a matter of how limited or expansive our imagination might be. Like Lovecraft, we might stop at fear, or like Borges, we might hold all possibilities in magnificent tension, open our eyes, and say, *Well met by moonlight, stranger.*

That is a gift—one of seven gifts that speculative fiction has for us in this dark hour. Often sold at bookstores as "science fiction and fantasy," sometimes as horror, sometimes snuck into the shelves of "literary" fiction, *speculative fiction* simply means wonder stories. Fiction that speculates, that asks improbable questions, that indulges curiosity, that climbs back down the ladder to look at the strange thing that is approaching from behind, to face it without fear, to face it like Theseus facing the King Horse, holding out a lump of salt. These are the stories we need right now, and I want to talk with you about *why,* and what healing and opening of our hearts and imaginations might be possible if we allow it. We live in a time when we are being asked to accept stories told by people whose hearts are famished and grinchlike, stories that make us smaller; we are in such need of stories that make us *bigger*, stories that empower us to imagine larger worlds than the cages we have been constructing for ourselves. Stories that help us imagine that the fence between us and the King Horse is no insurmountable barrier, and that all the fences and all the walls between us and our many kindred on this earth are unworthy of our respect, that we needn't heed them, that it is better to break them, or tumble them, or clamber over them with a lump of salt in our hand or a canteen of water, with a blanket to offer warmth, with ears ready to hear another's story.

As I write this, we are enduring the long night. Our people are ill and dying of a new disease. Our societies, at home and abroad, are beset by fascism—a shadow that, like Sauron's in Mordor, has found new opportunity to take shape and grow again. Climate change sends devastating heat waves, forest fires, and hurricanes to our shores. At every hour, faces on television and voices on Twitter are telling us to *fear, fear, fear*, like the drumbeat of our heart going too fast. And tragically, because death or extinction is *too* terrifying, because disease and ecological disaster are too frightful, we turn our fears on each other instead. Those *others*, they are what we must fear, our leaders and too many of our storytellers insist.

Against that drumbeat of fear, I write this book—as a love letter to science fiction and fantasy and as a letter of hope to you, dear readers, and I am writing it in 2020. It has been a long night. A cold night. I am in search of stories to warm us, *eager* to share stories that warm us. How we make it through this long night together will be dependent on the stories we tell and the stories we are willing to hear. Facing each other across the fire with our backs to the long dark, we need to share and hear wonder stories. And we need to hear them *well*, understanding the gifts of hope tucked inside these tales like trinkets or treasures tucked inside nested Russian dolls. Here, I'll show you what I mean. Come closer to the fire. Let's talk. Let me share with you these gifts.

CHAPTER TWO

TO GAZE INTO ELVEN EYES

WHAT DID BORGES' NARRATOR SEE WHEN HE AND the alien met, face to face, each looking into the eyes of the other? The first gift that we find in speculative fiction is the encouragement that we can climb back down the ladder and turn to the other with wonder rather than fear. The second gift is what happens at the meeting of the eyes.

In the film *Cloud Atlas,* there is a scene where an American lawyer has decided to shelter a Maori stowaway who has fled a life of slavery, in his passenger cabin aboard a ship bound for California. At dinner with the captain, he smuggles meat under the table and shares it later with the Maori. As he watches the man gulp down the food, starving, the lawyer asks, "How did you know I wouldn't turn you in? How did you know I would help?" The Maori meets the other man's gaze, points to his own eyes, then to the lawyer's. And he says, "All you need."

The philosopher Emmanuel Levinas proposed in his book *Totalité et Infini* that something remarkable occurs when we meet the eyes of the other. When two people have a face-to-face encounter and neither avoids the other's gaze, there is an intimacy that occurs. When I look into the eyes of another person, someone who is not-me, who is in fact different from me, who may have a different gender, religion, race, or class from my own—when I look into her eyes and see her looking back, there is an implicit "demand" in her gaze.

The demand is that I recognize her as akin to me. In this meeting of our gazes, we are both human. In this moment, I can recognize that she loves, hopes, fears, and desires, even as I do. That gaze bridges, briefly, our separateness and our aloneness. In other words, when I meet her gaze and she meets mine, her eyes communicate, implicitly, the demand that I respond to her as to a fellow and equal human being. It is a demand for ethical behavior: for just and compassionate treatment of the other.

This is why we ask others to look us in the eye so that we can see if they are communicating the truth to us. It is harder to lie (not impossible, alas, just harder) when you are gazing into the eyes of the person you're lying to. It's also why a hierarchical caste system in which society's lowest layers consist of "untouchables" is often paired with a cultural restriction on eye contact across castes. When you don't meet the eyes of untouchables, you are less likely to perceive any demand that you treat them justly, equally, and compassionately. Thus, you are less likely to respond, and the system is less likely to change. Similarly, Gandhi's project of *ahimsa* (nonviolence) was about facing the oppressor assertively but non-aggressively, eye-to-eye, making it difficult for the oppressor to avoid your gaze—in short, making it difficult for them to deny your essential human kinship.

In *Cloud Atlas*, the woman Sonmi-451, born a clone and a slave, sparks a revolution when she speaks of the interconnectedness of all human lives, across all social conventions and across all of time:

> To be is to be perceived. And so to know thyself is only possible through the eyes of the other. The nature of our immortal lives is in the consequences of our words and deeds that go on apportioning themselves throughout all time. Our lives are not our own. From womb to tomb, we are bound to others, past and present, and by each crime and every kindness, we birth our future.

SONMI-451, IN *CLOUD ATLAS*

In science fiction and fantasy, the other, the alien, the stranger, might come to us in any guise and in any shape. We might meet a girl who is also a dragon, or a girl who is mother to dragons. We might meet a person with pointed ears, or encounter another living soul who gazes at us out of a faceplate of metal. We are invited to hear their stories, to feel their feelings, to know their struggles. In his essay *A Defense of Poetry*, Percy Shelley suggests that imaginative stories train us to experience "sympathy" for others—that, in fact, all empathy begins with imagination: with the imaginative act of identifying with the other and picturing to ourselves what it would be like to experience and feel what they are experiencing and feeling.

What these stories teach us—these wonder stories—is that there is not only wonder but also the possibility of kinship when we meet the gaze of the other—or when we hear their story. We are each of us enclosed within a single mortal body. In various ways—in the union of lovemaking, in gathering around a small fire lit against the winter dark, in the sharing of bread with those who hunger, and in the telling and hearing of *stories*—we attempt to heal that aloneness.

To cure our essential solitude, we might even yearn to partake in a family that is as large as a species. Or larger: we might try to partake in a kinship that includes other life on Earth. We have seen a gorilla cuddle a kitten or a housecat on the edge of a pool play games with a dolphin; we have seen animals of different species bond and then weep at the other's passing. In all our bigotries—which lock us inside cages in our minds, to shrivel and shiver there alone—we forget that there is no shared hue, nor even any quota of shared DNA, that is required in order for us to be kin. Only mutual wonder at each other is required for that, only compassion.

Science fiction and fantasy help us imagine what it might be like to perceive ourselves as members of a family that is spread across a universe. That is a profound gift these stories offer us, if we are willing to accept it. So profound, so life-changing, that it brings tears to my eyes as I write. As a man of faith, I confess that when I read biblical wonder tales, this is the same revelation I find there, as well: a story about God, as the One who is *most other*, meeting our eyes, responding to our cries of pain—to our sorrow and our suffering—with his own, and with his love. In those wonder stories, on the Cross, God gazes at us and invites us to gaze back; he who responds to our pain with his love asks us to do likewise, responding to *his* pain with *our* love. In the same way, all the others who we

encounter in any of a thousand and one tales of wonder—
or the others we meet in those wondrous moments that
disrupt our own daily lives—demand our response to their
pain, to their implicit plea for kinship.

Will we look away?

Or will we answer?

As we walk across this planet heel to toe, continually
falling and catching ourselves, perhaps the strangest of all
Earth's animals—if our consciousness and sentience is
more than just a burden, if there is a gift in it, surely this is
that gift: that we have such capacity, such opportunity, to
gaze into the eyes of the other and see neither eater nor
thing to eat—not something to fear or something to
subdue, use, or devour—but one like ourselves, whatever
the shape we meet them in. There are people who bemoan
that the processes of evolution make our existence an
accident, but I have always found that complaint to be
both irrelevant and irrational, no matter one's beliefs.
Many children are accidents, and on the level of the wild
and unpredictable combination of DNA, from the mortal
perspectives of human parents, all children are accidents,
beloved accidents, unforeseen arrivals, others whom we can
neither imagine nor anticipate until they are here. In what
we call the "accident" is the wild gift, the joyous gift, the
encounter with the other whom we did not expect. We
choose to regard the other as marvelous or monstrous,
depending on whether we welcome or reject the wild gift.

All our wonder stories, both sacred and secular, are
about this encounter, because in our hearts, the encounter
with the other and the possibility of unexpected love and
unexpected union is both the scariest and most awe-

inspiring story we have to tell. It is the scary and wondrous tale that we desire to live. We put it in our books to make it real, to remind ourselves that it *can* be real. It is a story that requires our bravery, like the bravery of Borges' narrator at the end of that tale.

CHAPTER THREE

A DOOR TO ADVENTURE

THE EYES ARE "WINDOWS TO THE SOUL," IT IS SAID; the eyes of the other are more than windows—they are doors. Doors to adventure. And unforeseen adventure is very much what science fiction and fantasy deal with and train us for.

Gene Wolfe once wrote a novel entitled *There Are Doors*, and that title seems to me an excellent introduction to our tradition of wonder stories, which are all about doors. At the beginning of this book you're reading right now, Borges' narrator stood at a door—the door to a strange home. Readers of speculative fiction may be familiar with many such doors. In C. S. Lewis's *The Lion, the Witch, and the Wardrobe*, Lucy steps through a wardrobe door into a land of eternal winter on the other side. In the opening pages of *Three Parts Dead*, the first novel in Max Gladstone's Craft Sequence, the mage Tara Abernathy, just graduated, is booted from her academy world and tossed out of a door in the sky. She plummets toward the earth, using her magic to slow her descent. In Garth Nix's *Sabriel*, the door is the First Gate between life and death. The story opens with the necromancer's daughter attempting to resurrect a friend's pet rabbit. She steps into the river of death and approaches the First Gate. Gene Wolfe's *The Book of the New Sun* opens with Severian confronting a locked gate that becomes a symbol of his exile; Madeleine L'Engle's *A Wrinkle in Time* opens with a stranger's knock at the door of Meg's house in the middle of a storm; Ursula K. Le Guin's *The Left Hand of Darkness* begins with the envoy Genly Ai observing the construction of a gate; the action of *Star Wars* opens with a fleeing spaceship being drawn into the hangar bay door of a much larger vessel, followed by a scene in which a door on the captured ship is blown open to let in Darth Vader and a flood of stormtroopers. Bastian Balthazar Bux darts in through the door of a bookshop at the start of *The Neverending Story*. In *Doctor Who*, each companion finds that the real story of their life begins at the door to the TARDIS. And *The Hobbit* opens with a stranger coming to the door—Gandalf the wizard, arriving unexpectedly to invite Bilbo the hobbit to go on an adventure. For Bilbo, that round green door of his house in the hill is a doorway inward, to comfort. He routinely steps inside and relaxes into a comfortable, upper middle-class life. When he refuses the adventure at first, Gandalf marks a rune on the outside of his door. This rune both tells the traveling dwarves where to find Bilbo so they can whisk him away on that adventure—and it changes the meaning of the door. By scratching the rune into the wood, Gandalf alters the door from a doorway into comfort to a doorway outward to adventure. In a few more scenes, Bilbo will in fact go running out that door in such a hurry to adventure that he will leave behind his hat and his handkerchief. And the reader will go running out with him.

These are all "threshold texts"—narratives in which a threshold is crossed at the start of a tale. As a reader, when I open a book to the first chapter, I stand at the doorstep of a story, a story written by a stranger and populated with strangers and perhaps with stranger things than any I have known. There at the threshold, like a vampire, I have to be invited in. The threshold text is the mechanism by which a storyteller invites me into the book. Or, for a less vampiric metaphor, maybe both the fictional character and I, the reader, might be carried over the threshold like a bride, right into a new life.

The importance of this crossing of the threshold has been noted by Maureen Quilligan in *The Language of Allegory*, Joseph Campbell in *The Hero with a Thousand Faces*, and Andrew Hallam in "Thresholds to Middle-Earth." That threshold is both *invitation* and *context*. The invitation excites the reader, intriguing the mind or getting the blood pumping. Simultaneously, the context relaxes the reader, by providing just enough information for us to get "lost" in the story. It's a lure. It's a door that just *has* to be opened, like the door of a wardrobe in an empty house or the door to a red mansion on a hill when the rain is pouring. Like Gandalf, the storyteller will have marked the door with some rune, some clue that hints at the adventure awaiting us on the other side.

Yet, once I *do* step through that door, I have no way of knowing what may happen. It is like stepping into a stranger's house for the first time—whether as a welcome guest or an unexpected one (like the dwarves who visit Bilbo or like Mrs. Whatsit coming to tell Meg and her mother in the middle of the night that there *is* such a thing as a tesseract), or even as a burglar, an intruder—like Borges' narrator searching the house for some comprehension of its occupant or like Bilbo at the doorway into the mountain, into the dragon's lair. When I step into the stranger's house—or out of my door into an open world populated by strangers, by strange wonders and strange perils—I have no idea how my story will go.

Oh, I can trick myself into thinking that I do: that I know the formula of the genre, that I know how the tale will proceed and what will happen in it, that I know that I will drive to work, chat with colleagues over a coffee break, then drive home, kiss my wife and children, help make dinner and help eat it. But any number of unexpected arrivals or chance encounters might throw my formula completely ajar. I might have a car accident. I might encounter someone dying on a sidewalk. I might bump into an old friend long parted, who I never expected to see again, who has changed in ways perhaps neither of us expected. Other things might happen. There might be a protest in my city; I might be moved to join it. There might be a pandemic. That long dormant volcano on the horizon might decide this is a good day to wake up. There might be dragons. Who knows? "It's a dangerous business, Frodo, going out your door," Bilbo counsels his nephew. "You step onto the road, and if you don't keep your feet, there's no knowing where you might be swept off to."

That is what good stories are all about—the encounter with the unexpected, and the fact that this encounter is an invitation to adventure. Those who read voraciously often confess that there are a handful of books that have "changed their life." Indeed, how could it be otherwise? It is in the nature of an adventure that something is *ventured*, something is risked and something might be gained. Whether on a journey with fictional characters or in an encounter with the flesh and blood people who live outside the covers of the book but who might enter our lives no less unexpectedly, there is always the risk and the opportunity that we will change. That is the most fearful and the most wondrous thing about all stories, about all relationships in which you share and live your stories together: that possibility. In the end, when you close the book, or when you return home from your strange encounters of the day, you might find yourself looking about at your life with new eyes:

> *And the end of all our exploring*
> *Will be to arrive where we started*
> *And know the place for the first time.*

T. S. ELIOT, *FOUR QUARTETS*

Gandalf's rune scratched into the door is the third gift that speculative fiction has for us. It is the gift of risk, the gift of adventure, the gift of change. It is the gift of having change thrust upon you within the relative (but perhaps illusionary) "safety" of a book. It is the gift of seeing change as a call to adventure. It is the gift of learning that there is pleasure and not only peril in answering that call.

Stories can mark new runes on the door of our lives. Doors open *into* our home and *out to* the world, inward to the past and outward to the future. A story can change our past and our future—not the actual facts of events but what they *mean*. Stories can help us reinterpret and retell and, going forward, *relive* or live differently the adventure that we are on. Because of course this life *is* an adventure. We just trick ourselves into thinking it isn't. Into thinking that difference can be ignored or thrust aside where it doesn't need to be looked at. Into thinking that your daily routines and your habits of thought are stable, predictable, and will not be disturbed. But it's only a trick, a glamor that we cast without even knowing that we're doing spellcraft. Just beyond our sight, there are always dragons. And nearby, hidden from us in plain sight—in places where we refuse to glance or forget to look—there are always people we aren't seeing but who are nonetheless *there*. People rendered invisible. People we perceive as other. People who are lovely and suffering. Science fiction and fantasy remind us that *not* seeing what's around us, not treating our lives as an adventure full of possible encounters, is not actually safe; it is only *sad*.

CHAPTER FOUR

WHEN HAGGARD'S CLOCK

STRIKES THE RIGHT TIME

THERE IS A SKULL ON THE MANTEL AND IT IS laughing. Well might it laugh, for our planet tilts ever more swiftly as time rushes by, dragging us all with it to shatter us in the end against the wall of death. The adventurers in the story gaze up at the talking skull in dismay; there is something they badly need to know. They have a unicorn with them imprisoned inside the body of a woman, a human woman, and they have sworn to reunite her with her people. A terrible guardian stands in their path—the Red Bull—and they've been told that the only way to the Red Bull's lair and, past him, to the unicorns is to walk through King Haggard's clock, perhaps into a hidden tunnel or down a secret stair, when the clock strikes the right time. But *when* will the clock strike the right time?

> The glass over its face was broken, and the hour hand was gone. Behind gray glass, the works could barely be seen, twitching and turning as fretfully as fish.

PETER S. BEAGLE, *THE LAST UNICORN*

Sometimes King Haggard's clock strikes four at midday, or thirteen o'clock just before dawn, or the noon hour at sunset. Here, then, is the door to adventure—but how to open it? This dry, desiccated skull holds the secret, perhaps, if he can be made to talk. The magician strikes at last upon a suitable bribe: a memory of wine, more precious and delicious to the skull than the substance itself, because the skull has no palate or tongue, but it *remembers*. In return, the skull gives them the key to the mystery:

> If you wait for the clock to strike the hour, you'll be here till you're as bald as I am. ... When I was alive, I believed—as you do—that time was at least as real and solid as myself, and probably more so. I said 'one o'clock' as though I could see it, and 'Monday' as though I could find it on the map; and I let myself be hurried along from minute to minute, day to day, year to year, as though I were actually moving from one place to another. Like everyone else, I lived in a house bricked up with seconds and minutes, weekends and New Year's Days, and I never went outside until I died, because there was no other door. Now I know that I could have walked through the walls. ... The clock will never strike the right time. Haggard scrambled the works long ago, one day when he was trying to grab hold of time as it swung by. But the important thing is for you to understand that it doesn't matter whether the clock strikes ten next, or seven, or fifteen o'clock. You can strike your own time, and start the count anywhere. When you understand that—then any time at all will be the right time for you.

PETER S. BEAGLE, *THE LAST UNICORN*

And then, even as King Haggard rushes to stop them, shouting "Smash the clock!", the adventurers dart through it, not to a hidden stair after all, but simply *through it*; one of them experiences the passage through the clock "as though she were a dryad and time were her tree." And then, they are simply *elsewhere*. In a place where no clock tolls the hour, where there is no schedule or calendar, just the *moment* with the full richness of its possibilities for action, for heroic deeds or fearful ones, for victory or defeat, for joy or grief. They have their chance.

* * *

J. Alfred Prufrock, in T.S. Eliot's poem, measures out his life in coffee spoons, day after day after day, growing old until he feels Time pressing at his back, scythe in hand. He lives bricked up in the house of *chronos*, which is "clock time," the relentless tick-tock of the day to day, the time of Empire: the disciplined march of military boots, exacting schedules, and adherence to tradition. Every moment planned and expected. All possibilities anticipated, documented, and known. *Chronos* is the relentless march toward death in a world locked and closed, where the only sanctioned and proper interpretation of what your life means and can be or become … is Caesar's, or Big Brother's, or Mussolini's. An orderly, disciplined, hierarchical world. A constricted and restricted world, an intolerable world, an unjust world. In that world the trains always run on time.

But there are other kinds of time. Even J. Alfred Prufrock, too timid to dare eat a peach, knows this in his heart; the poem is *The Love Song of J. Alfred Prufrock*, after all. He yearns for love. Love is one of the ways you can strike the right time, one of the ways you can step through King Haggard's clock. Creating is another, and so is play. So is wonder.

In the early years of this era, the Greek-speaking Christians who wrote the New Testament conceived of three kinds of time; to do so, they borrowed language from the Greek philosophers, transmuting it through the wild alchemy of their wonder stories about a messiah and a miracle-worker and a God enfleshed. For them, there were *chronos, aion,* and *kairos. Chronos* is the clock time that has Prufrock in its thrall and that Haggard tries to escape when he smashes the clock. But there is also *aion*, eternity, God's time. Time without beginning or end, an eternal present. In *The Consolation of Philosophy*, the theologian Boethius imagined that God exists in just such an eternal present, able to see all of time at once, all pasts and all futures simultaneously. For Boethius, God is able to reach from *aion* into our *chronos*. He is able to touch our inexorable clock-time world with his finger and shatter our expectations and schedules and limitations as easily as a fist might shatter a glass. For him, the deity's arrival in the world is the unpredictable event, the impossible that cannot be planned for or scheduled. It is a *kairos*, an unexpected moment that stops *chronos*. Frank Kermode, in his book *A Sense of an Ending*, calls *kairos* the "silence between the *tick* and the *tock*." It is when the pendulum stops and you hold your breath, because the timeline you thought you were in—the story you thought you were reading or living—suddenly has the potential to change, right out from under you. Sometimes we translate *kairos* "the right time," "the right season," "the occasion," or "the opportunity." It's the moment when you step through the clock.

Wonder tales are concerned with *kairos*; they offer us an invitation to the Event, which is a term philosophers Jacques Derrida and John Caputo use to describe the encounter with the impossible, an unexpected encounter that can shake us to the core. Wonder tales—*The Last Unicorn; The Lion, the Witch, and the Wardrobe;* Borges' story *There Are More Things;* even the wild tales in our Bible, from the parting of the Red Sea to the Resurrection, tales we often attempt to tame and domesticate, penning them inside sermons—all these tales dramatize the coming of the impossible, the Event that creates previously unforeseen possibilities and opportunities for how we understand not only everything that has yet *to happen* but everything that *has happened*. Any hour, any instant, can potentially be "the right time"; any time can be a *kairos*, because the impossible Event, the opening of the invisible door, is not something you put on an itinerary. It is something that happens unexpectedly, as a disruption or shattering or melting away of *chronos*. The most evocative description of *kairos* that I have ever read is Madeleine L'Engle's; she calls *kairos*

> … that time which breaks through *chronos* with a shock of joy, that time we do not recognize while we are experiencing it, but only afterwards, because *kairos* has nothing to do with

chronological time. In *kairos* we are completely unself-conscious and yet paradoxically far more real than we can ever be when we are constantly checking our watches for chronological time. The saint in contemplation, lost (discovered) to self in the mind of God is in *kairos*. The artist at work is in *kairos*. The child at play, totally thrown outside himself in the game, be it building a sandcastle or making a daisy chain, is in *kairos*. In *kairos* we become what we are called to be as human beings, cocreators with God, touching on the wonder of creation. This calling should not be limited to artists—or saints—but it is a fearful calling.

MADELEINE L'ENGLE, *WALKING ON WATER*

It *is* fearful, because when the *kairos* occurs, it means opportunity—opportunity that is risky and dangerous and requires bravery. Will the adventurers leap through the clock, not knowing exactly where they will land, possibly arriving to face the menace of the Red Bull, that supernatural monster of sinew and flame? Will Lucy, finding no back to the wardrobe and feeling a winter chill across her fingers, press forward through the fur coats and then through branches of fir and cedar, with no foreknowledge of what she might be stepping into? Will the new companion take the Doctor's hand and step into the alien interior of the TARDIS? Will the Israelites dare to cross between towering walls of water after God has parted the Red Sea? Will the women facing the empty tomb dare to believe that death has been rolled back and their friend walks and breathes even at that moment in the garden? At the moment of *kairos*, the adventurer is presented with a risky choice. If they seize the opportunity, then potentially the future will be written very differently than they had anticipated. Not only that: the past will be *re*written. Not the facts of the past, but what those facts *mean*. Once the Children of Israel walk through the midst of the sea and enter the desert as a free people, their past lives of slavery and oppression will be understood differently. What their past slavery *means* to their identity will change. The stories they tell of their past will now be told from the perspective of a free people. That companion who stepped into the TARDIS and will now travel across time and space will never understand her life the same way again. And in the Christ story, the Resurrection is an event that changes both future and past—"redeeming" the past—because if all God's children rise to eternal life, then the death and suffering and loss of the past, which has still happened and is still real, *means* something different than it did before Mary Magdalene saw an empty tomb.

Just like Peter S. Beagle's characters leaping through the clock or the Israelites walking between two parted walls of ocean water, the reader can be an adventurer. The reader encounters an impossible Event in the story and has the opportunity (*kairos*) to change how they understand the story and what the story means and what could possibly happen in the story. And as we draw analogies between the story in the book and that other story that we are telling ourselves about our own life, we have the opportunity to infer and imagine and find new interpretations of what *our* story means. When wonder, creation, or love stops time like Neo stopping bullets in *The Matrix*, anything becomes possible. We might find ourselves making love, lost in another's arms, in another's eyes, in another's heart, turning upside down what our life has meant or could mean. We might find ourselves gazing at a night full of stars and seeing them, *really* seeing them, for the first time. We might find ourselves making a ridiculous, magnificently foolish choice—like falling in love, or scrapping a career and starting a new one or none at all, or beginning a journey, or making a child. Anything might be possible. We might find ourselves conversing with a stranger whose story has drawn us outside of time—a stranger that our culture might have otherwise separated us from, but here, now, in this chance encounter, in hearing their story, we find kin where we didn't expect, and everything changes. We might find a *kairos*, an opportunity, to break chains—ours', or others.' To take up a cause, to find ourselves (to our own shock) marching in the street besides people we don't know who are nonetheless our brothers. Prufrock wouldn't dare to eat a preach and he certainly won't dare to talk to a woman he likes; time has him chained up, has had him chained up a long time. He still thinks he can find Monday on a map, yet he *knows* in his heart. He grieves. That is a man who needs a fairy tale. That is a man who needs a TARDIS or a parting of the sea. Though perhaps … perhaps he would be too timid to answer the call to adventure.

But perhaps he would.

It is a mistake to underestimate the people we meet, whose inner lives we do not know, whose stories we haven't yet heard.

* * *

The particular gift of speculative fiction is not only that it can unshackle us from time—any story can do that, as long as it has a little wonder in it, or more than a little love—but that it also grants us a vocabulary for *talking* about time and adventure, grants us new ways of imagining and conceiving of our relationship to time and our relationships to each other, so that we can go on unshackling ourselves after we have closed the book.

Science fiction often plays with relativity, exploring what it is like to travel through time at different speeds from one another. I will never forget how moved I was the first time I read this passage in *A Left Hand of Darkness*, in which the exile Estraven realizes how much his lover Genly Ai is an exile, too—Genly who has traveled to Estraven's planet from another:

> Long since in Ehrenrang he had explained to me how time is shortened inside the ships that go almost as fast as starlight between the stars, but I had not laid this fact down against the length of a man's life, or the lives he leaves behind him on his own world. While he lived a few hours on one of those unimaginable ships going from one planet to another, everyone he had left behind him at home grew old and died, and their children grew old ... I said at last, "I thought myself an exile." "You for my sake—I for yours," he said, and laughed again.

URSULA K. LE GUIN, *THE LEFT HAND OF DARKNESS*

Science fiction translates Einstein's theories into story, into lived experience—lived vicariously, yet felt as real. Fantasy plays its part, too, in unmooring us from time; at each return to Narnia, the children find that time has passed differently there (and unpredictably). In Gene Wolfe's *The Book of the New Sun*, there is an encounter at the top of a tower near the end of the world, with a reddened and dying sun in the sky; there, a mad scientist suggests:

> Look about you—don't you recognize this? The castle? The monster? The man of learning? Surely you know that just as the momentous events of the past cast their shadows down the ages, so now, when the sun is drawing toward the dark, our own shadows race into the past to trouble mankind's dreams.

GENE WOLFE, *THE SWORD OF THE LICTOR*

Dr. Talos's exclamation is fanciful, implying that we tell Frankenstein stories because of a Frankenstein event that will happen in the future—but perhaps there is *something* to it. After all, is that perspective any stranger than the attitude toward time that we now have, the attitude the talking skull parodied, our confidence that we might find Monday as if on a map? As a metaphor, at least, Dr. Talos's whimsical explanation of how the future affects the past makes me think about what a *kairos* can do to our understanding of history. The call to adventure doesn't just alter our future; it forever changes how we tell and remember our lives, the narrative of who we have been until that point. When you fall in love, when you experience a religious conversion, or when you meet a stranger whose words shock you and alter how you think about life, you look at your past through new eyes. This is one of the purposes of the wonder story—to catch us

31

between the *tick* and the *tock*, to stop us at the bottom of the ladder in the red mansion. What we learn from the wondrous encounter and what choices we make because of it—that is up to us. But the opportunity, the *kairos*, when for just a moment, the impossible breaks through the chronological march of time and expectation—that is the fourth gift that science fiction and fantasy have to offer us. The fourth gift is that these stories can open King Haggard's clock.

CHAPTER FIVE

EVERYBODY HAS A SECRET WORLD

INSIDE OF THEM

IN *THE ODYSSEY*, ONE OF THE OLDEST OF OUR wonder stories, an adventurer in the guise of an old man, who has battled and sailed and wandered his way home through encounters with many strangers (some of them kind and some of them perilous), arrives at last on his own doorstep—as a stranger himself. His hair is white and bedraggled. His hands are wrinkled, his eyes bleary with age and with the weight of too many painful memories. He comes pleading for scraps of meat, for wine or a drink of clear water. He comes with a story.

Emily Wilson says this of him, in her introduction to her translation of *The Odyssey*:

> There is a stranger outside your house. He is old, ragged, and dirty. He is tired. He has been wandering, homeless, for a long time, perhaps many years. Invite him inside. You do not know his name. He may be a thief. He may be a murderer. He may be a god. He may remind you of your husband, your father, or yourself. Do not ask questions.

Wait. Let him sit on a comfortable chair and warm himself beside your fire. Bring him some food, the best you have, and a cup of wine. Let him eat and drink until he is satisfied. Be patient. When he is finished, he will tell you his story. Listen carefully. It may not be as you expect.

EMILY WILSON

This is a thing I love about Homer. Everyone and every thing has a story; one need only look. That cup that was given to you as a guest-gift and now has a crack in it—it was once held by such and such a hero. That shield was forged by such and such a smith. That warrior there, at home he tends herds of horses whose manes flow like foam on the night sea. And that warrior over there, his people keep beehives that drip the tastiest honey west of the mountains. In Homer's story-world, as in our own, everything is brimming and overflowing with life, with both a past and with potential for a future. Seen this way, all things and all people are, to borrow Sappho's phrase, "golder than gold." The tragedy of war in the *Iliad*, the tragedy of violence, is the reduction of people to mere objects, when not even objects are *mere* objects. Anything might flower into a wild future, but we human beings who follow Ares' scream out onto the battlefield, or who, like Penelope's suitors, grab up what we can and swill to our belly's content while others starve—we deny the potential futures, we burn the books, we cut short the stories that are all around us.

The fifth gift that science fiction and fantasy have for us is to remind us that these stories are *there*, that *everything* around us is wild with life and full of possibility. The

Doctor in *Doctor Who* travels across all of time and space, always in a breathless rush to see *every*thing, to talk with every creature. In the episode "The Power of Three," one of the Doctor's companions accuses him of always *running away*. Surprised, he answers:

> I'm not running away. But this is one corner of one country on one continent on one planet that's a corner of a galaxy that's a corner of a universe that is forever growing and shrinking and creating and growing and never remaining the same for a single millisecond, and there is so much—so much to see, Amy. Because it goes so fast. I'm not running away from things; I am running to them. Before they flare and fade forever.

THE DOCTOR, IN *DOCTOR WHO*

The beautiful gift in the story of *Doctor Who* is that, to the Doctor, everyone—absolutely everyone, in every species— is worth seeing and talking to. In another episode, "A Christmas Carol," we find this scrap of dialogue:

> THE DOCTOR: Who's she?
>
> SARDICK: Nobody important.
>
> THE DOCTOR: 'Nobody important.' Blimey, that's amazing. D'you know, in 900 years of time and space I've never met anyone who wasn't important before.

At its best, science fiction and fantasy empower us to imagine, to perceive, that not only is no one in the wide universe *unimportant*, but also each person is *wondrous* and worth "running to." It's something we forget or fail to believe, but wonder stories challenge us to suppose that it might be true. In Neil Gaiman's *The Sandman*, Barbara says after a friend's funeral:

> Everybody has a secret world inside of them. All of the people of the world, I mean everybody. No matter how dull and boring they are on the outside, inside them they've all got unimaginable, magnificent, wonderful, stupid, amazing worlds. Not just one world. Hundreds of them. Thousands maybe.

BARBIE, IN *A GAME OF YOU*

Barbie is unwelcome at the funeral service, which is a gray and grim event; the family of her deceased friend insist on deadnaming her. "It's Alvin," they insist. When the service is ended and the relatives in black have faded from the cemetery, Barbie gets out a stick of lipstick in her friend's favorite hue. With it, she crosses out the deadname on the tombstone and writes beneath it her friend's name, *Wanda*.

People get frightened of the "unimaginable, magnificent, wonderful, stupid, amazing worlds" that exist inside of others. They miss out on the wonder and joy of knowing one another. They condemn and reject without ever listening to the other's story of who they are, of what their particular adventure has been. This causes a poverty of the imagination, a famishing of the soul, a shriveling of the ability to love. Seeing others and hearing their stories, we might be moved to love them. Or, loving them, we may crave hearing their stories. But we cannot truly *love* them if we have no interest in their story.

Near the end of my own *Ansible: A Thousand Faces,* the reader encounters a character who has grown a thousand eyes, one for each of the worlds she has visited over the course of her long existence:

> The artisan's arms are bare to her shoulders, and with a shock I realize there are dozens of eyes set in her pale skin from shoulder to elbow and elbow to wrist. A few of the eyes are lidded but moving as if they dream. Many are open and watching her work. They are all different, and none of them are human, but they are beautiful. One, multifaceted like a bee's and bamboo green, gazes up at the earth. Another, round and amber and slitted, gazes at me … There are otherworldly eyes in her cheeks and running down one side of her neck like a tattoo, and one the size of her fist right in the center of her forehead, gazing at me but not reflecting me, reflecting instead the tossing boughs and scarlet fronds of a red forest many light years from here. But the two eyes she has had longest, one to either side of the bridge of her nose, are soft with grief and patience.

ANSIBLE: A THOUSAND FACES

At a crucial moment in the story, the reader is invited, for a moment, to see through her thousand eyes:

> I open all of my eyes … I feel I can see the universe, full of people to love. Each of my eyes sees a memory, a world, a heart mine might touch.

ANSIBLE: A THOUSAND FACES

And in my novel *No Lasting Burial,* Yeshua, who is both deity and man, gazes into the eyes of a dead man who needs forgiveness; for an instant, Yeshua remembers the fullness of what it was to be God before his incarnation:

> "I looked into his eyes," Yeshua whispered. "And he looked into mine. And I could see, oh I could see. Myself, reflected in his eyes. I remembered." The smallest shake of his head, his eyes glassy with pain and wonder. "I could breathe out a billion stars. All that life and beauty. Everything so beautiful—and so fragile. Everything dying and being born. And the sky, always getting bigger, always bigger. Too small to hold all the things I love. It's slipping away now," Yeshua breathed. "All the suns and all the worlds and all their peoples. A moment ago, I could see them. See all of them. For just a moment—"

No Lasting Burial

Too small to hold all the things I love. The universe is vast, and yet each person in it has a universe inside them. Like the TARDIS, people are so much bigger on the inside. As I suggested early in this book, how we choose to encounter the other is a matter of how limited or expansive our imagination might be. If inside every person there are worlds we might know, if every person is important, if every person has a story, if all of humanity is a *library*, then just by existing, just by being born, you have been handed a library card to the greatest treasurehouse of wonder tales and adventures and mysteries and close encounters and love stories that there has ever been. Yet in our bigotries or in our complacency, we train ourselves to throw that card away! Or only to check out books *from one shelf.*

Science fiction and fantasy stories try to remind us of our access to and coexistence with this library, by making the universe itself—all of time and all of space—their topic. We see each other through a glass darkly; it is our greatest tragedy. But if we choose, if we are brave, if we do not close our eyes, then our ability to hear each other's stories is our great opportunity and our great hope. That is the *kairos* before us. Each time we open a science fiction or fantasy novel, we are learning how to sit down and listen to a stranger's tale. And in our lives outside the storybook, any time we choose to do *that*, to sit with the stranger and listen to their tale, King Haggard's clock might strike the right time and we might step into adventure. Isn't that so worth doing?

* * *

The adventure has to be accepted deliberately; it has to be chosen. It is easy to stay at home, even when beset by wonders, by wizards and tales of dragons and hoarded treasure. Even after singing all night with the exiled dwarves from another land in *The Hobbit*, Bilbo could have chosen to stay in bed the next morning, to remain a comfortable bourgeois Baggins who never sought adventure, never took a risk, and certainly never invited strangers to tea. In the same way, the talking skull in *The Last Unicorn* warns the adventurers that while he was alive, he never went outside until he died, because he couldn't see the door. Speculative fiction teaches us that *there are doors*, but then it is up to each of us whether to step through them.

In the essay *J.K. Rowling and the Limits of Imagination*, written in response to a beloved author's transphobic rants, Nathan J. Robinson laments:

> I still think, and will always think, that these books are a dazzling feat of human inventiveness. J.K. Rowling can imagine almost anything. She can imagine fantastic beasts, enchanted castles, oozing potions, explosive spells. The creator of Harry Potter could imagine the most marvelous fictional universe in children's literature—yet she can't imagine the inner lives of transgender people. She cannot imagine her way to questioning the deepest injustices of our time, and she cannot imagine why people are offended when she says hurtful and ignorant things about marginalized people.

NATHAN J. ROBINSON

Sadly, it's not enough just to read a wonder story or even to write one. The fact that we have tales about fellowships of diverse races working together to destroy a weapon of mass destruction in the form of a Ring, or stories about people from different classes and genders working together to resists fascists and keep schoolchildren safe, is not enough by itself to grow our imaginations and enlarge our hearts. We have become too used to enjoying spectacle as an isolated experience, separate from our daily lives, or to regarding science fiction and fantasy stories as an *escape* rather than a *kairos*, so that we miss that break in chronological time that provides the occasion to reassess where we are and what we are doing and why. We have become lazy readers—and yes, sometimes, lazy writers, too. If we choose to treat these stories as if we are merely tourists on a cruiseliner in outer space, we will miss the adventure. We will miss the *kairos*, the opportunity. We will remain unchanged. Any wonder story can be *The Neverending Story* to us, but unless we permit that, all books, no matter how marvelous and astonishing their content, will remain merely "safe," as Mr. Coreander warns Bastian Balthazar Bux.

Books are not meant to be *safe*, science fiction and fantasy least of all! Each of these books has a secret world inside it, and each of their characters has a secret world (or many) inside them. These books needn't be *only* an escape from our world, because they can also operate as a fresh jolt to our imaginative batteries, reviving our capacity for perceiving our own world, for seeing what's around us and *who* is around us, and what encounters and choices might be possible. Let's each of us *not* make J. K. Rowling's mistake. Let's not neglect the gift. If we can imagine worlds where people ride on the backs of titanic sandworms across endless desert or a world where a teenager can walk into the waters of death and ring magical bells to silence the ravenous dead, we can also imagine and choose to see and hear the secret worlds inside of all the wondrous, important, unexpected people who live and breathe all around us.

When we open a wonder story and begin reading, a rune is marked on our door. But, like Bilbo Baggins, we can choose either to ignore it or to run from our comfortable home out to join the strangers we have met, even at risk, even if we are not quite ready, even if we have left our hat and our handkerchief behind. Will we answer the call to adventure that we find in the eyes of the other?

CHAPTER SIX

WATER INTO WINE,

FOR ONE WILD MOMENT

IF WONDER STORIES ARE NOT *MERELY* AN "ESCAPE," then what are they? If the indolent choice is to treat them as a mere trip to the Colosseum, as the "circuses" in *panem et circenses* (bread and circuses), an entertainment to while away the hours and avoid engaging with an increasingly difficult and grim world—if the stories are not *merely* that, then what might they be to us? What fire might burn in our hearts as we read?

> These tales say that apples were golden only to refresh the forgotten moment when we found that they were green. They make rivers run with wine only to make us remember, for one wild moment, that they run with water.

> G. K. CHESTERTON, *ORTHODOXY*

When I first read that essay of Chesterton's as a very young writer, I adopted it at once as my mission statement for what I wanted to do as a storyteller, for what I wanted my stories to do to their readers: to make the river run with wine so that the reader might remember, for one wild moment, that the river runs with water. It was not escape I sought but *restoration*. Revival. Resurrection. One of my favorite paintings, by Ursula Vernon, depicts a tiny dragon curled like a seahorse on a red maple leaf. I used to gaze at that painting in such quiet joy. Even today, that artwork resurrects for me a hundred childhood moments when the trees were red and full of wonder.

Like the boy Theseus who ran out to talk with the King Horse, not in boldness but in wonder, I want to see the world fresh and full of possibility again. Like the characters in Homer, I want to see a secret world inside every cup and in every mountain grove. Wordsworth expresses this longing in one of his sonnets—

> *The world is too much with us; late and soon,*
> *Getting and spending, we lay waste our powers;—*
> *Little we see in Nature that is ours;*
> *We have given our hearts away, a sordid boon!*
> *This Sea that bares her bosom to the moon;*
> *The winds that will be howling at all hours,*
> *And are up-gathered now like sleeping flowers;*
> *For this, for everything, we are out of tune;*
> *It moves us not. Great God! I'd rather be*
> *A Pagan suckled in a creed outworn;*
> *So might I, standing on this pleasant lea,*
> *Have glimpses that would make me less forlorn;*
> *Have sight of Proteus rising from the sea;*
> *Or hear old Triton blow his wreathèd horn.*

William Wordsworth

—but unlike Wordsworth, what I want, and what Chesterton describes wanting, isn't only the experience of some vast magical spectacle embedded in our world, an old god rising from the sea, like those we read about; what *I* want is to see everything around me infused with magic, with life, with possibility. This desk on which I write—I rarely *see* it, though I sit at it every night. Yet it is a *wonder*. It has a history. It was a gift from a friend. Touching its smooth surface, I might recall what a Herculean labor it was to get it up and down stairs! This broken handle on the desk drawer, there was a *moment* when it broke. And this desk has a history I don't even know about, that I could be curious of, wondering. It was once in the house of my friend; before that, elsewhere; once upon a time, it was a tree. What tree, and where? How old of a tree? What centuries did it see flit by? What lovers' trysts did it hear, what soft whispers in the night beneath its branches? What rainfall did it feel on its leaves, long before my great great grandmother was born? Oh my readers, our tragedy is *not* that we do not see Proteus rising from the sea; our tragedy is that this writing desk has ceased to be as magical, as wondrous, as Proteus rising from the sea!

Our fears lock us away from each other and they also *dull our eyes*. But for one wild moment, we might see the world as if for the first time—and, in that moment, we might be open to all of it and to anyone in it. In George MacDonald's *Phantastes*, the narrator Anodos rests one night in the forest, after a terrifying episode, in the sheltering arms of a beautiful woman. In the morning, he wakes and finds that she was a beech tree:

With the sun well risen, I rose, and put my arms as far as they would reach around the beech-tree, and kissed it, and said goodbye. A trembling went through the leaves; a few of the last drops of the night's rain fell from off them at my feet; and as I walked slowly away, I seemed to hear in a whisper once more the words: 'I may love him, I may love him, for he is a man, and I am only a beech-tree.'

GEORGE MACDONALD, *PHANTASTES*

Reading of that beech tree, no beech tree will ever again be *ordinary* to me, because all beech trees are wondrous, full of life, "golder than gold." Whatever tree my desk came from, it wasn't *ordinary*. Whatever river it grew beside, that river ran with *water*. What could be more wondrous than that?

CHAPTER SEVEN

UNSTOPPABLE HOPE

IN *THE LORD OF THE RINGS*, WHEN FRODO IS HELD captive like a princess in a tower, and Samwise Gamgee rushes to his rescue, Sam comes to a dead end. He is alone in the dark. He has reached top of the tower, but there is no door. He cannot find his beloved friend. Feeling defeated, he sits down. His torch goes out, and he sits in the dark.

> It was quiet, horribly quiet … and he felt the darkness cover him like a tide. And then softly, to his own surprise, there at the vain end of his long journey and his grief, moved by what thought in his heart he could not tell, Sam began to sing. His voice sounded thin and quavering in the cold dark tower: the voice of a forlorn and weary hobbit … He murmured old childish tunes out of the Shire, and snatches of Mr. Bilbo's rhymes that came into his mind like fleeting glimpses of the country of his home. And then suddenly new strength rose in him, and his voice rang out, while words of his own came unbidden to fit the simple tune.

In western lands beneath the Sun
  the flowers may rise in Spring;
the trees may bud, the waters run,
  the merry finches sing.
Or there maybe 'tis cloudless night
  and swaying beeches bear
The Elven-stars as jewels white
  amid their branching hair.

Though here at journey's end I lie
  in darkness buried deep,
beyond all towers strong and high,
  beyond all mountains steep,
above all shadows rides the Sun
  and Stars for ever dwell:
I will not say the Day is done,
  nor bid the Stars farewell.

J.R.R. Tolkien, *The Return of the King*

And there, beyond all hope, he hears a second voice, thin and faint, singing with him. Frodo's voice. And Sam hurries to unbind and free his friend.

Later, as he and Frodo crawl across the volcanic plain of Mordor, their hopes wane again. The journey is hard and beset by foes; the very air chokes you as you breathe it. Volcanic fire makes the horizon a hellscape, and the ash overhead deprives you of daylight. And then, one night, while Frodo sleeps, Sam peers up at the darkened sky:

There, peeping among the cloud-wrack above a dark tor high up in the mountains, Sam saw a white star twinkle for a while. The beauty of it smote his heart, as he looked up out

47

of the forsaken land, and hope returned to him. For like a shaft, clear and cold, the thought pierced him that in the end the Shadow was only a small and passing thing: there was light and high beauty for ever beyond its reach.

J.R.R. TOLKIEN, *THE RETURN OF THE KING*

There with Sam, as a reader, I am breathless at that beauty he sees in the sky, a light in dark places when all other lights go out.

Similarly, in a very old tale of horrors and wonders—the *Inferno*—after 33 cantos of crawling through level after level of hell, hearing the screams and sobs of the lost and damned, Dante follows his guide Virgil through a tunnel in the rock and out of the underworld at last:

> *"So that I saw some of the lovely things*
> *That are in the heavens, through a round opening;*
> *And then we emerged to see the stars again."*

DANTE ALIGHIERI, *INFERNO*

That sight of the stars is the last line in the *Inferno*—the escape from hell, the hope of heaven. That is where the poem ends. Gene Wolfe writes an homage to this scene in his novel *The Knight*; in the scene, Sir Able, a boy transported from our world to a fantastical realm, has just fought dragons deep inside a volcano. Now he is climbing out, hand over hand, at great labor, sweaty and hot, carrying an injured man to safety on his back. And just as Able feels too weary to continue:

"I felt a cool wind … I looked up, trying to see where it was coming from and how tough the slope was going to be up above, and I saw stars. I will never forget that, and I can shut my eyes right now and see them again. You do not know what stars are, or how beautiful they can be. But I do."

GENE WOLFE, *THE KNIGHT*

For one wild moment, the stars have been made new for Sir Able. These are not the stars we walk beneath in the cool of the evening in the city, on nights when we forget to glance up. They are not the stars that we have forgotten how to see. They are the stars *Dante* saw, climbing up out of the horrors inside the earth. They are the stars Sam caught a glimpse of, high above the fumes of Mordor. They are the stars the soldiers of Troy behold the night before battle in the *Iliad*:

> *And so their spirits soared*
> *as they took positions down the passageways of battle*
> *all night long, and the watchfires blazed among them.*
> *Hundreds strong, as stars in the night sky glittering*
> *round the moon's brilliance blaze in all their glory*
> *when the air falls to a sudden windless calm…*
> *all the lookout peaks stand out and the jutting cliffs*
> *and the steep ravines and down from the high heavens bursts*
> *the boundless bright air and all the stars shine clear*
> *and the shepherd's heart exults—so many fires burned*
> *between the ships and the Xanthus' whirling rapids*
> *set by the men of Troy, bright against their walls.*

HOMER, *THE ILIAD*

About this passage, Bernard Knox writes, in his introduction to Robert Fagles' translation of the epic poem:

> These are surely the clearest hills, the most brilliant stars, and the brightest fires in all poetry, and everyone who has waited to go into battle knows how true the lines are, how clear and memorable and lovely is every detail of the landscape the soldier fears he may be seeing for the last time.

BERNARD KNOX

Before the walls of Troy, above the ash-choked plains of Mordor, glimpsed even from inside the dragon-haunted cone of a volcano, *there are the stars.* Those stars—they are the seventh gift these wonder tales have for us. The gift of hope.

* * *

In the film *The Shawshank Redemption*, Stephen King puts the words that follow into the mouth of an escaped convict, unjustly convicted, who spent decades digging a slow tunnel out of the prison with a rock ax the size of a spoon:

> Hope is a good thing, maybe the best of things, and no good thing ever dies.

STEPHEN KING

Hope. In the fourth episode of Neil Gaiman's comic series *The Sandman*, the lord of dreams visits hell, even as Dante did. He comes to win back something stolen, and because the denizens of hell are slow to part with it, he ends up drawn into a duel fought on the battleground of the imagination. It is a duel of stories, a duel of wonder tales, in which the demon Choronzon and the dreamlord Morpheus strive to outdo each other. Choronzon's tales are fantasies of annihilation, extinction, and entropy; Morpheus counters them with dreams of life and warmth. At last, confident he has won, the demon taunts the dreamlord:

> CHORONZON: "I am anti-life, the beast of judgment, I am the dark at the end of everything. The end of universes, gods, worlds … of everything. And what will you be *then*, dreamlord?"

> MORPHEUS: "I am hope."

To that, Choronzon can find no answer. The duel ends. *Abandon all hope, ye who enter here* may be written on the gates of hell, but the Sandman who pours dreams through his fingers onto the eyelids of mortals has made of it an empty threat. Hope is the storyteller's province and method, no matter where the storyteller travels.

Elsewhere, paraphrasing G. K. Chesterton, Neil Gaiman suggests,

> Fairy tales are more than true: not because they tell us that dragons exist, but because they tell us that dragons can be beaten.

> NEIL GAIMAN

Wonder stories dramatize that idea by pitting we small, foolish mortals against *dragons*—against threats and dangers magnified a hundredfold by the power of the imagination. Against Choronzon's imagined "beast of judgment, the dark at the end of everything" is set hope that is frail yet unstoppable. Wonder stories strengthen us against our next dark hour by teaching us that stars still burn bright and clear above the darkness, that cities burnt can be rebuilt, that plagues can be quenched, that dragons can be beaten, that there is always one more chapter in the neverending story that is our lives.

* * *

When the long night is at its darkest, there are two ways to look for hope. The first is to look for eucatastrophe, for rescue at the eleventh hour. *Eucatastrophe* is a term coined by J.R.R. Tolkien, the "good destruction," the opposite to the *catastrophe* that ends a tragedy. In a tragedy, the character whose life had seemed on the verge of great joy or vast destiny suddenly finds everything overturned. The Book of Job opens with such a tragedy; Job is a wealthy man who reveres his God and conducts his affairs with integrity, and then one afternoon, unexpected, "out of the blue," he is visited with woe upon woe:

> And there came a messenger unto Job, and said, The oxen were plowing, and the asses feeding beside them: And the Sabeans fell upon them, and took them away; yea, they have slain the servants with the edge of the sword; and I only am

escaped alone to tell thee. While he was yet speaking, there came also another, and said, The fire of God is fallen from heaven, and hath burned up the sheep, and the servants, and consumed them; and I only am escaped alone to tell thee. While he was yet speaking, there came also another, and said, The Chaldeans made out three bands, and fell upon the camels, and have carried them away, yea, and slain the servants with the edge of the sword; and I only am escaped alone to tell thee. While he was yet speaking, there came also another, and said, Thy sons and thy daughters were eating and drinking wine in their eldest brother's house: And, behold, there came a great wind from the wilderness, and smote the four corners of the house, and it fell upon the young men, and they are dead; and I only am escaped alone to tell thee.

JOB

That is *catastrophe*—the abrupt reversal of events from good to terrible. For Oedipus, it is the revelation of his parents' identities. For Ahab and his hapless crew, it is the fatal clash with the White Whale.

For readers, catastrophe can serve any of several functions. It can provide a *memento mori*, a reminder that we, too, are mortal; that the wheel can turn; that, in Solon's phrase, no man may be judged happy until his life has ended and can be seen in its entirety; that, in Donne's phrase, we need not ask for whom the bell tolls; it tolls for us; death comes for us all. Or it can provide a *catharsis*, a cleansing of the turmoil within us achieved by the sharing of tears—a way of letting out all the fear and anger and pain we have pent up. Or it can provide a simpler relief, a breath of fresh air, as we realize that *we* are alive, even though the characters are dead. The angel of death has brushed our cheek with its wing for just a moment, in a story, yet we have come away breathing and whole. "There but for the grace of God go I," we each breathe, and go about our day with renewed appreciation for the fact that we get to live it.

*Eu*catastrophe provides a different function. Its purpose is not to instill solemnity but to kindle joy. Tolkien used the word to explain what occurs at the end of *The Lord of the Rings* when all hope appears utterly lost, and then—as if by chance, but in truth made possible by the past deeds and kindnesses of the characters—suddenly, unexpectedly, the Ring is destroyed; the characters and their world are rescued (though not all are unscathed). Where catastrophe is the sudden reversal of events from good to terrible, eucatastrophe is the sudden reversal of events from terrible to very good. It comes as unexpectedly as the abrupt deaths of all Job's family and all his flocks, but while catastrophe casts Job to the ground in sackcloth and ashes, naked as the day he was born, eucatastrophe picks us up, clothes us, pours wine into our thirsting mouths, and provokes us to dance and laugh, like David dancing naked before the Ark after his people are saved. Like Mary Magdalene weeping with joy as she gazes up into the face of a friend and teacher she had thought dead, on Easter morning. Hearing such a story, there is a shout in our hearts; in Tolkien's phrase, we are "wounded with sweet words, overflowed." Speaking from a religious perspective, Tolkien writes:

> [*Eucatastrophe*] produces its peculiar effect because it is a sudden glimpse of Truth; your whole nature chained in

material cause and effect, the chain of death, feels a sudden relief as if a major limb out of joint had suddenly snapped back. It perceives ... that this is indeed how things really do work in the Great World for which our nature is made.

J.R.R. TOLKIEN

Such tales appear not only in comfortable living rooms in more comfortable years when you might sit and read a book, but also during the long night, in the mouths of the suffering in many places at many times, when stories of hope and wonder are fashioned at great need for peoples beset by cruelty or poverty or by the sadism or callousness of their fellow human beings. West Africans enslaved on islands in the Caribbean or on plantations in the American South once told stories about flying back to Africa. In some of these tales, a wonder worker would visit their hovels—an old man with skin like theirs, who spoke their own language, who remembered the stories of their lost home, and who would teach them how to fly. It would be a long flight back across the ocean, but the sun would be bright on their feathers.

Eucatastrophe is not always messianic—it can also be a self-fashioned escape, like that in *The Shawshank Redemption*. And eucatastrophe is what the characters in Marvel's *Infinity War* yearn for when this conversation happens:

> DR. STRANGE: I went forward in time ... to view alternate futures. To see all the possible outcomes of the coming conflict.
>
> PETER QUILL: How many did you see?

DR. STRANGE: Fourteen million, six hundred and five.

TONY STARK: How many did we win?

DR. STRANGE: …One.

There might be only 1 in 14,000,605 timelines in which we survive, but *this might be that timeline*. That is the hope for eucatastrophe, a kind of hope that burns brighter and brighter and, like Han Solo piloting through an asteroid field, cares nothing for the odds.

* * *

The first way to look for hope is to look for eucatastrophe, rescue at the eleventh hour. The second is to look for creation.

I will tell you what I mean. To do this, I want to take you back, briefly, to one of our truly ancient stories of creation—the Genesis story—and share with you something that many Western readers miss. Something beautiful. When we read that story in the Old Testament, that tale of wonders in which a universe is *spoken* into being, as if the universe itself is a tale God is telling, we usually read it imagining that God in that story is performing *creatio ex nihilo*, making something "out of nothing." First there was nothingness—an empty void; then, *bam*, there was something. That's a Roman idea dating back to the fourth and fifth centuries, an idea that was attractive to the descendants of Empire, inheritors of a culture obsessed with power and omnipotence. But the story did not originate in that Empire. It is very old. It is a story written for a people whose lives were more precarious, who were recalling a time of exile, a time when their ancestors were nomadic, alone with their God in the wilderness. There is no *creatio ex nihilo* in the original Hebrew. Their word for "create" was *bara*, which is something entirely different. *Bara* suggests taking pre-existent, raw materials and shaping them into a new thing that has purpose, use, and beauty. For example, when you take a hollow reed and poke holes in it and turn it into a flute, you are doing the kind of creation that is *bara*. When you take a rock and carve it into a statue, that is *bara*. When you take twelve people of diverse classes, traditions, and motivations, and weld them into a team of apostles, that is *bara*. When you take dust and form it into a human being and breathe life into it, that is *bara*. The poet John Milton, having read his Old Testament in Hebrew, described God creating worlds out of "his dark materials" in the epic *Paradise Lost*.

That idea of the empty "void" or nothingness isn't original to the story, either. We often translate *tohu vavohu* that way, but the Hebrew suggests not a void but a desert. In that ancient tale, the universe before God touches it is not empty like a blank space but empty like a lifeless desert. A desert isn't *nothing*. It is just a dry place where the land shifts and few plants take root, where there is less form and less life. The ancient Hebrews were the agrarian descendants of a people who had once crossed deserts. Reading Genesis, they might have pictured the wilderness beyond their farmlands and imagined God taking all that emptiness and making it fruitful, filling it with light and life and green, growing things. For that Hebrew reader, this story of creation implied incredible hope—because a desert is not a dead space. A desert is raw materials. *That* story of the universe begins with a desert place bursting into sudden life and potential, and their story of humanity begins with life breathed into something that a moment before was only dust. In other tales they told, collected in our Bible, the God who called to the desert goes on creating and re-creating the world, throughout all of time. God calls water out of the rock, makes springs bubble up in desert places. God visits the desolate with new life— from Naomi in the book of Ruth to Elizabeth in the book of Luke. God visits the bitter, the grieving, or the hard-hearted and turns them into apostles, prophets, healers, teachers, and even kings who dance naked before the Ark in an extremity of joy. In biblical wonder-narratives, *bara* is what God does with each of us, taking the "dark materials" of our hearts and making all things new.

I am so moved by that ancient yet timeless narrative of a God who stirs the desert and makes a whole universe out of it. Deserts, no matter how bleak, are not forever; no matter how formless and desertlike a life might seem, it may yet flower again. That is also what my pen name means. More than a pen name, *Stant Litore* is my life motto, the words I have inscribed on the door of my life since I was a teen. You can find my legal name on the copyright page of this book. It's no secret. *Stant Litore* is not a concealment for me but a daily unforgetting of a story I hold in my heart.

The phrase is Latin, and it comes from the Roman epic *Aeneid*. In that tale, while the city of Troy burns in defeat after a devastating war, Aeneas leads the survivors fleeing toward the shore. The sky above and behind them is dark with ash and lit by flames. There are distant screams. Ahead of them, someone calls back: "Hurry! Hurry! The ships stand at the shore!" In Latin, *stant litore puppes!* "The anchor is already drawn up! Hurry! The ships are here to take you away!"

As far as the refugees from Troy know, this is the end of their world. Where there were homes and gardens and markets, there is nothing now but smoke and ash. Where there was a city, there will now be ruins and desert. What they *don't* know is that once they embark on those ships and cross the sea, they are going to found Rome, a civilization that will last for thousands of years. They have a breathtaking future ahead of them that they can't even imagine. That doesn't change what they have lost, but their loss does not define the totality of their future. Ash is very fertile. An entire civilization might be born out of the ashes of their city, an entire universe might be summoned forth out of a desert. That story of impossible hope, of endless creating—of *bara*—speaks deeply to me.

Eight years ago, I sat vigil for long months beside a hospital bed while my infant daughter Inara fought for her life. We were cautioned, her mother and I, that she might not make it through her first year. That if she did, she would be unlikely ever to see, stand, or walk. All of these, she has done. She is a fighter, and she has done the impossible. That is the meaning of *her* name; she is named for a crew member on the fictional spaceship *Serenity*, whose captain said of his crew, "We have done the impossible, and that makes us mighty."

In *Lives of Unstoppable Hope*, my own memoir of my family's darkest hour, I wrote this:

> "Now my daughter is improving, and we are on the other side of that time together. Yet those nights by her bed are recent in my heart, and they hurt. I don't know what this past year has meant, only that the love I now hold for those I call my own is fiercer than anything I have ever felt. I have learned that hope, which I had thought small and delicate like a moth in the night, can be hard as steel, a blade with which you cut your way through a press of moaning and hungry foes."

The story of the past eight years might so easily have been written differently and more darkly, but Inara's survival and her conquest of life has been a reminder to me that the possibilities of tomorrow are always uncharted, that tomorrow is always being created anew. I try to live my life continually unforgetting that no matter how desolate or how long the night, the ships still stand at the shore—in Latin, *stant litore*.

This is different from the hope for an eleventh hour rescue—because in this case the eucatastrophe, if it comes, may come long after you and I are here to see it; none of the refugees from Troy will be alive when the city of Rome is founded. But it does not come "too late," because this hope is based on seeing yourself as a chapter in a story that is larger than both you and the pain that besets you—a tale of persistent creation. In *Lives of Unstoppable Hope*, I wrote:

"It is a strange comfort, perhaps … but it is a mighty comfort. Not a single one of us is alone or insignificant, because we each walk among a mighty crowd of fellow witnesses to the world's pain, fellow exiles, fellow grieving ones, others who, poor in spirit, striving to make peace, have gone on hungering for justice and for *rightness*. We walk alongside David and Deborah, Samuel and Samson, Martin Luther King, Jr. and Susan B. Anthony and Harriet Tubman, alongside people who have struggled and won, and among people who have struggled and lost. Their struggle is ours, and ours, theirs. We are all on pilgrimage, all of us exiled together and walking the long walk toward a better country. And that can be a source of hope! Of unstoppable hope. Not of the weak, delicate butterfly hope I once imagined, but of sword-blade hope, the hope you carry at your side and wield … Strong as steel though slender, that hope is what we use to cut our way through.

We can live lives of unstoppable hope.

We must.

We are all pages in the vast story that God is reading, that we and God are writing together. The road is dark and the wind is shrieking: yet we will walk hopefully and fiercely. We will remember the story we are in. We will remember our song in the night; we will rejoice and be glad; we will be salt-seasoning and light in the dark. Let the winds howl as they will; the storm may slay us, but it will never, *can* never unmake us or defeat us. Be still, waves. Be still, wind. We— my readers and I, and David and Moses and Gandhi and Buddha before us, and who knows but perhaps Clone 776-A5 and Martok of New Mars and as yet unimagined saints after us—will walk across this sea. And some evening yet, in this life or the next, there will be a shore, and a better country. We will keep walking toward it together, through one night or a thousand."

We may not live to see the morning, but the night *will* end. And so we carry our torches high, because hope is not just a thing for one individual, but for a people.

I think this is the hope that Samwise Gamgee feels when he gazes up at that one star twinkling in the sky. His hope at that moment is not specifically that he and his master will succeed, but that the darkness and the desert is as temporary as they are, and the consolation that visits him is deeper than the hope for rescue:

> His song in the Tower had been defiance rather than hope; for then he was thinking of himself. Now, for a moment, his own fate, and even his master's, ceased to trouble him.

J.R.R. TOLKIEN, *THE RETURN OF THE KING*

This is the hope not that it will soon be day for *you*, but that day *will* come again. In Tolkien's *Silmarillion*, the warrior Hurin stands alone against a horde at sunset, and at each blow of his ax he cries, "*Aurë entuluva!* Day shall come again!" Even if the night lasts ten thousand years, *aurë entuluva,* day shall come again.

These words were found written on the wall of a cellar in a Holocaust concentration camp:

> *I believe in the sun even when it is not shining.*
> *And I believe in love, even when there's no one there.*
> *And I believe in God, even when he is silent.*
>
> *May there someday be sunshine*
> *May there someday be happiness*
> *May there someday be love*
> *May there someday be peace.*

I pray that you and I will never find ourselves in a night as long or an hour as dark as that. But if we ever do, may the wonder stories we read prepare us for it. May they give us the hope we need to "stand at the shore."

* * *

In this way, storytelling is an act of survival. In Leslie Marmon Silko's *Almanac of the Dead*, a people are exterminated, leaving only two children alive. The two children flee through the woods, carrying with them the written stories of their people; to fend off starvation, they eat the stories. The stories of their people keep them fed and alive as they run.

In *Ansible: A Thousand Faces*, an ancient time traveler says:

> By story and song, we hold back the dark. Grandmother and her australopithecines knew this, I think. They used to gather under a great baobab on the edge of the savanna and warble together while the dusk fell. The first human song, entering the world at the fall of night. All their eyes shone with it. They linked hands. They sang. It is really always the same song, across all of time, in infinite variations, but always
>
> *the flutter of hope and the beat of the heart,*
>
> the song I sang softly to my son, as a lullaby, when he was in my womb and later, when I carried him bundled in my arms and I was dusty with walking across Syria, my feet

cracked, the skin on the back of my hands cracking, my voice cracking. The song Sahira sang, using another tune and other words, when she sang to my baby in a broken house in a broken city, when she kept us alive and there was only she, and me, and my son left in the world. The song I hummed at my son's cradle in Quebec City, while snow fell soft and silent against the glass window in his small bedroom. While I pressed my hand to his tiny chest to feel the drumming of his heart. The song I sang to my great-great grand-daughter and her husband, when Sahira and I met them as if by chance in a park of alien trees with pink blossoms, on the campus of the Université de Nouveau Quebec on a colony world orbiting Proxima Centauri, my descendant a laughing bride and I only a nameless and happy old woman in a park who enjoyed singing to the young. Oh, how I sang! How I sing! The pneumavores fall toward me with eternal slowness, never to arrive; behind them, flames burn motionless—as the fire Moses saw in the burning bush—though if there was time their fire would consume the ship; and I sing. I sing that song that drums in my breast when I think I stand immersed in silence. Heartbeat and hope, loudest in the dark. The heartbeat song that overtakes my whole body when Sahira is in my arms and I in hers, and we are loving. The song that has been sung and chanted and shouted and whispered in a million languages, in a million bodies, on a million worlds, the first song and the last song, the song that is: *We are here, we are alive; nothing will part us; what need have we of a sun in this dark, for there is this fire in our hearts!*

ANSIBLE: A THOUSAND FACES

We are part of a larger story. Such hope grants not resignation but agency and creativity. During the long night, Frodo tells Gandalf, "I wish these things need not have happened in my time." Gandalf replies, "So do all who live in such times, but that is not for them to decide. All we have to decide is what to do with the time that is given us."

Such hope frees our most creative selves to act in whatever moment we find ourselves; it packs each encounter not only with peril but with possibility, with *kairos*. As the world darkens, we *venture*. "In the face of overwhelming odds, I'm left with only one option – I'm gonna have to science the shit out of this," says the marooned astronaut in Andy Weir's *The Martian*. Facing climate change, human beings tell stories of solarpunk, dream of arcology cities, invent economic ways to sweep the ocean for trash. Science fiction, especially, teaches us to solve problems, even overwhelming ones. That's one of the implicit promises in the genre—that if we can imagine a thing, we can create it. Arthur C. Clarke imagined satellites; *Star Trek* imagined cell phones and tablets. If we can imagine a more just community, we can create that, too, if enough of us believe in the story to make it real. Neil Gaiman tells a lovely parable of this in *A Dream of a Thousand Cats*, in which a wandering Siamese cat preaches her vision that if a thousand cats all dream on the same night of a world where cats are titans striding the earth and human beings are small as mice, then such a world will come to exist. Other cats scoff, remarking that *no one* will ever succeed in getting a thousand cats to dream the same dream. Yet one or two believe, and pass the story on.

This seventh gift that wonder stories have for us is that they invite us to see the universe as larger than we usually think it is, and our own part in it as smaller yet also more significant than we think—because we are all living a neverending story that began long before we were born and will continue long after we are gone, a story that we take part in writing. We are a storytelling species, and there is always a new chapter being created. Despair is the belief that we are on the last page of the book, and that we are there alone; it is the relinquishing of our ability to speculate about our future, believing we have no part in that future; that is why speculative fiction can be curative. Wonder stories seek to break and shatter that despair. That is the gift we need to share with each other during the long night.

CLOSING REMARKS:

WE NEED LARGER STORIES

I HAVE SUCH JOY AT THE BOOKS THAT ARE ON OUR shelves now. I remember hungering as a much younger man for stories other than those I could see there. I wanted stories of wonder, and I wanted stories of others' lives, stories of other worlds. I wanted to crew starships along with people of every gender, ethnicity, religion, and class. I want to time travel with hijabi mages and see the first pyramid raised. I wanted to sail a dhow along the coast of Zimbabwe and help black mariners recover an artifact from a sorceress. I wanted to drink water changed into wine on the other side of the world and see people raised from the dead. I wanted to charge into battle on tyrannosaurback with a strike force of elite nonbinary swordfighters. I remember how difficult it was at one time to even find a person who didn't look like *me* on the cover of a book, let alone inside it. To this day, I don't think there has ever been an American edition of Ursula K. Le Guin's Earthsea novels with non-white characters depicted on the covers—even though almost none of the characters in the books are white.

But change, long fought for and hard won, is coming. Thanks to shifts both in our culture and in the publishing and entertainment industries, from the box office success of *Black Panther*, to international writers and writers of color taking the Hugo Awards, to the Own Voices movement, there is *so much more* on the shelves than there once was. The starships are getting crewed more diversely, in dozens of science fiction novels. That dhow sailing to confront a sorceress beyond Zimbabwe—Milton Davis has written that for us, in *Changa's Safari*. Rebecca Roanhorse has given us a Navajo monster hunter to help a small town find a missing girl, in *Trail of Lightning*; Lois McMaster Bujold has given us a disabled scion of a military family who ventures into the universe to seek his fortune, in the *Vorkosigan Saga*; Nnedi Okorafor has given us a tale of a young Himba woman setting out to study mathematics on another planet, only to find her ship attacked in *Binti*; Kim Stanley Robinson has given us an alternate history in which the Black Death wiped out Europe and the scientific exploration of the universe is conducted by Muslims, Buddhists, and indigenous peoples, in *The Years of Rice and Salt*; and there are not only dozens but hundreds more such stories. The elite nonbinary sword-companions who ride tyrannosaurs haven't been written just yet, so maybe I will write them—but so much of what I yearned for, and so much of what I never knew I *could* yearn for, is here. And there is so much more to come. You and I have opportunity now to hear more stories other than our own, so many invitations to adventure—to the *greatest* adventure, which is to encounter and love other lives that sojourn beside us on this earth. I am so grateful, and so ready to listen and to hear what my neighbors have to say, to find out what wonders and horrors *they* have seen in this tragic universe—and what it might be like to walk by their side.

* * *

And I have so much to learn. Even as white writers try to find new ways to understand and tell stories of pandemics, crises, and apocalypses, indigenous writers remind us pointedly that their peoples have already survived an apocalypse, that each of their storytellers already lives in a post-apocalyptic world. Our mainstream culture has adopted science fiction and fantasy, taking it as a diversion and an escape, getting drunk on summer blockbusters (before the pandemic, at least) and desiring ever more spectacle. But to marginalized storytellers, speculative fiction has been an opportunity to imagine futures and possibilities that are other than the present; speculative fiction can be a way to reconstruct and newly construct community—a way to find unstoppable hope in a grim time. Surely their tales are stories the rest of us need to hear.

At this hour, as *everyone*, mainstream and marginalized, is hit (albeit disproportionately) with the impacts of a pandemic, a recession, and ecological crisis, we have neither summer blockbusters to turn to nor the luxury any longer of treating wonder tales as mere popcorn experiences. Even the most privileged at this dark hour can feel the cold brush of death as it passes down the hall. This is a time to remember how much we *need* wonder stories, how badly we need to speculate about alternate futures. When this time passes, if we strive only to "go back" to how things were, to the injustices and unsustainable complacency that constricted our society before the pandemic, then we will be the most pitiable of fools. We need to imagine better, improbable, impossible futures—and then act to *make* them possible.

It would be easy for me to say here, *go tell larger stories, tell more inclusive stories, tell wildly imaginative stories that turn this world we know completely upside down and inside out, wonder stories that dare us to imagine that we can do that!* And I do say that. I teach writing classes; that is one of the things I say. And yet, in this hour, for those of us who are safest, who have the greatest privilege, it is even more important to *hear* stories than to *tell* them. Dear readers, have we not become, increasingly, a culture of people who spend more of our time talking and soapboxing and less of our time reading, listening to, and sharing stories? This will not do. In our generation, we have to become better at hearing each other's stories, at accepting the thousand invitations to adventure. How do you heal the world? I have no idea how to answer that question in full, but I do know that one of the things we will need along the way are millions and millions of compassionate, skilled *readers*, by which I mean skilled and open-hearted hearers of each other's stories. We need people who will hear stories from diverse others (fictional others and then *real* others)—people who approach everyone's story as eager, curious hearers and readers. What we need in this long night is good readers and good stories.

We need to hear the imaginative, potent stories that are already being told by those voices that don't have megaphones to shout the loudest, by the voices that aren't always the most comfortable for the privileged to hear, by the voices that are throwing open all the doors. Some of our fellow human beings are telling larger stories than the ones we are being spoonfed each day; we need to listen. We need to hear them. There are adventures we are being called to, encounters long delayed yet all the more important with each passing day.

* * *

I said earlier that storytelling is an act of survival. It can also be an act of intimacy, if we consent to it. A letter, a speech, a narrative, words spoken to your ears: any of these might invoke a moment of intimacy and relay the other's demand for love, kinship, and justice. In *An Experiment in Criticism*, C. S. Lewis contends that reading a great story can be one of those acts—like love or just action—that permits us to experience union with others:

> "We want to be more than ourselves. Each of us by nature sees the whole world from one point of view with a perspective and a selectiveness peculiar to himself... In love we escape from our self into one other. In the moral sphere, every act of justice or charity involves putting ourselves in the other person's place and thus transcending our own competitive particularity... The primary impulse of each is to maintain and aggrandize himself. The secondary impulse

is to go out of the self, to correct its provincialism and heal its loneliness. In love, in virtue, in the pursuit of knowledge, and in the reception of the arts, we are doing this… The man who is contented to be only himself, and therefore less a self, is in prison. My own eyes are not enough for me, I will see through the eyes of others. Reality, even seen through the eyes of many, is not enough. I will see what others have invented. Even the eyes of all humanity are not enough. I regret that the brutes cannot write books. Very gladly I would learn what face things present to a mouse or a bee; more gladly still would I perceive the olfactory world charged with all the information and emotion it carries for a dog. Literary experience heals the wound, without undermining the privilege, of individuality. There are mass emotions which heal the wound; but they destroy the privilege. In them our separate selves are pooled and we sink back into sub-individuality. But in reading great literature I become a thousand men and yet remain myself. Like the night sky in the Greek poem, I see with a myriad eyes, but it is still I who see. Here, as in worship, in love, in moral action, and in knowing, I transcend myself, and am never more myself than when I do."

C.S. LEWIS, *AN EXPERIMENT IN CRITICISM*

I yearn to hear more stories, and to tell the stories I hear— to tell and retell and pass them on—because in stories I encounter others who are so different from me and yet are human, just as I am. I want to hear everyone's story. I wish I had the time and immortality and patience to hear everyone's story. And like C.S. Lewis, I yearn also to know what the world sounds like to a whale or what it smells like to a wolf—to those *other* kindred to whom we, in our anthropocentrism, have done wrong and who may also have appeals to make to our compassion or justice, and experience and insight of their own to share, if we only knew to listen for it. I long to hear the stories of all the souls in the world who are not me. To see the universe with a thousand faces, and to treat the wearers of those thousand faces in the way we treat people when we have taken their stories into our hearts.

To encounter the other—in story, or in life—is a *kairos*, an opportunity, a moment of choice, where the enlargement of our hearts and the healing of our separation from each other is made suddenly, unexpectedly possible. In my own *Ansible: A Thousand Faces*, Rasha imagines humanity as a mosaic:

> All the moments of a life, all the moments of the life of humanity, every act of fear and each act of love, make a picture that can only be seen with a thousand eyes, a mosaic that only God or a time traveler can glimpse; there may come a night aboard a vast battleship above the earth when I can catch the briefest glimpse of it too—brief, in my periphery, out of the corner of my eyes. I am awed and terrified to think of it, for when that occurs, how will I bear it? How does *she* bear it, my Sahira? How is she not mad? How does she see what she sees and remain human? How does she see and still love? Or does she love so deeply *because* she sees, because she cannot see and *not* love? One night, I will know.

ANSIBLE: A THOUSAND FACES

A mosaic is made of many broken pieces of colored glass, yet the whole is as beautiful as it is broken. So, too, with humanity.

Reading and writing fantasy novels, we get to speculate about alternate pasts and alternate earths. Reading and writing science fiction novels, we get to speculate about alternate futures. Why should our futures be small, populated only by a select group? I would not wish to dwell in so small a future; I have C.S. Lewis's hunger for more experience and for deeper companionship with other living beings. Elizabeth Kerner, in her novel *Song in the Silence*, coined the term *ferrinshadik*: the longing for companionship with another sentient species. It is fitting for human beings to experience *ferrinshadik*, because once upon a time, we *did* have companionship with other sentient species. Even love. Each one of us carries neanderthal DNA in our genes. Maybe some part of us remembers. So of course we would write stories about bonding with dragons or running in primeval forests alongside elves, or wedding a Martian on the shores of a dead sea. But maybe our *ferrinshadik* and our loneliness is so much the greater because we now sever ourselves from so many of our *own* species. We are the lonely ones. It is a way in which we have wounded ourselves.

* * *

As I write this, I am also toiling gleefully at a manuscript for the first novel in a new science fiction series, *The*

Dakotaraptor Riders. One of the cultures we encounter in this new story regards it as vitally important for everyone's story to be heard. Sasha Nightwatcher explains:

> There's no justice on this planet but what we make. For Dmitri, raised by Ticktocks and abandoned by Ticktocks, justice was an objective thing. Your clock tells wrong or it tells right. Sometimes, the universe's clock is off the hour and has to be set right. Everything must be counted and accounted for, especially blood spent and spilled. But I am one of the humming people. Justice is not a matter of the hours told right but of songs finished, melodies made complete, tales that reach satisfying ends, and no teller's tale ending too soon. No matter how hard the story, you don't give up until it's told. When you see another trying to sing and they can't, you help them. If someone has no voice, you help them make a drum and you learn sign. If someone is captive, slaved by raiders, you break their bonds, take the gag from their mouth, and get them out into the free prairie where they can sing again. If red rain falls, you get everyone under shelter where the hum of their heartbeats can continue, however frightened and quick. You never give up, just as the Founder herself never gave up. You sing and you love and you hum with life until your very last breath, and you do what you can so others get to breathe and sing, too. *That's* justice, if justice is the word. That's the way of the humming people.

Those beliefs are written into the code of the nightwatchers, the dinosaur riders who take up the nocturnal defense of their people:

If our people are sick, we will find healers.
If our people are starving, we will find the herds.
If our people are captive, we will cut the ropes from their wrists.
If our people are fleeing, we will guard their passage
through cropland and prairie and wild forest.
If our people are silent, we will sing their tales.

And when one among this close-knit people perishes, it is the duty of the rest to tell their story:

We have to finish her song. Grandma Yaga requires a burial and a payment in song, a story of your life sung by those who remember you, in exchange for passage across the frozen prairie in her walking hut. If none remember you, if none continue the song of your life's deeds after you are gone, then you are left to wander in the endless frost, in an empty land whose blades of brittle, frost-rimed grass break at a touch. Empty but for other ghosts who wander there like you, silent and without song. Sometimes you hear Grandmother's cackling laughter in the stillness, her hut sprinting by on its raptor legs too quick to catch, no matter how fast you and the other ghosts run. We have to finish her song.

It is vital in Sasha's culture to make sure everyone's stories get told—even one's enemies' stories. No one, after all, wants a planet filled with ghosts. And that desire to ensure that the community hears each person's story—that is the true meaning of the name of their planet.

Their planet is named Peace.

* * *

I said I was writing a love letter to science fiction and fantasy and a letter of hope to you, dear readers. If you have found some hope in its pages, then I will have done my work well. May your nights ahead be filled with stories. At the bottom of the ladder, may you choose not to close your eyes. May you suffer *ferrinshadik*, the yearning to encounter and hear the other. Not only to see a dragon, but to sit and hear the tales of our brothers and sisters and others who have long gone unheard, who might share with us wonders more breathtaking than the flash of dragonscale in the sun, and sorrows sharper than any written on the edge of a blade in a fantasy novel. May you meet so many fascinating people that you could never have predicted meeting—so many people that when you meet Grandma Yaga at last and you ask her to let you ride in her walking hut across the ghost prairie, you will have *such* stories to tell her.

May you read and *read*—I have heard that in the early months of the pandemic, beset by fears and confusion, many in lockdown found reading difficult, concentration impossible. Oh, but stories are what we need most right now. Because by stories and song we hold back the dark. Because stories prepare us to welcome and hear the other. Because stories make rivers run with wine so that we will remember, for one wild moment, that they run with water. Because stories call us to adventure. In this long night, we crave rest and safety and yet have never needed adventure more.

We need bigger stories and bigger hearts. We need to let our hearts always be stretched larger by others' stories. This is how, together, we will make it to the other side of the night.

STANT LITORE
SEPTEMBER 2020

KHOVAKAA

THE CHARACTER ON THE COVER OF THIS BOOK IS Khovakaa, from the fictional world of Lauren K. Cannon's Dhuriiehm, appearing on the cover with the artist's permission. Lauren describes Khovakaa as "a deity for the unpleasant side of mother earth—decay and disease, all the foul parts we push away but occupy so much space in the world." Khovakaa seems a very fitting character to encounter in this year of the pandemic. I feel the thrill of both wonder and woe, seeing her gaze back at me from that painting; at her gaze, I want to tell stories even when beset by plague and fear, even in the mist above the swamp and beneath the dark that eats the stars.

I hope you will explore more of Lauren K. Cannon's art, because it is evocative, beautiful, horrific, and each painting is a door to adventures, whether dark or hopeful. You can find her art illustrating many books, and at:

www.navate.com

ABOUT THE AUTHOR

STANT LITORE WRITES ABOUT ZOMBIES, ALIENS, AND tyrannosaurs. He does not currently own a starship or a time machine but would rather like to. He lives in Aurora, Colorado with his wife and three children and hides from visitors in the basement library beneath a heap of toy dinosaurs, tattered novels, comic books, incomprehensibly scribbled drafts, and antique tomes. He is working on his next novel, or several. You can read some of his current fiction by looking up *Ansible*, *The Running of the Tyrannosaurs, The Zombie Bible*, or *Dante's Heart*—or the new series, *The Dakotaraptor Riders*, beginning fall 2020. However, venturing into these worlds may have unpredictable effects, and Stant offers no assurances that you will emerge from any of these stories unscathed. Best leave all non-essentials behind, take with you only what you need to survive, and venture into the books cautiously and ready to call for backup. Enjoy, and good luck.

www.stantlitore.com

IF YOU ENJOYED THIS BOOK...

I HAVE MORE FOR YOU TO READ.

My work on this book—and on my novels, too—has been funded by the generous support of my Patreon members. If you would like to join them in supporting my work and see previews of what I am working on next, you can do that here:

WWW.PATREON.COM/STANTLITORE

May your days always be full of good stories, may your ears always be open to the stories of others, and may your life be one of unstoppable hope.

* * *

I want to extend my gratitude especially to Olivia Wylie and Shoshanah Holl for their careful read of the manuscript and their thoughtful feedback, to Lauren K. Cannon for her art, and to Brady Stanton for the cover design.

MORE BOOKS

FROM STANT LITORE...

STANT LITORE

ANSIBLE

A THOUSAND FACES

ANSIBLE: A THOUSAND FACES

"MY MIND HAS TOUCHED THE STARS, WEARING A
THOUSAND FACES…"

In *Ansible*, 25th century Islamic explorers transfer their
minds across space and time to make first contact…and get
marooned in alien bodies on alien worlds. Along the way,
they encounter the most dangerous predator humanity has
ever faced. And that species knows where earth is. Now a
Syrian refugee, a thirteenth-century librarian, and a hijabi
shapeshifter from the far future must travel across space
and time to defend humanity from this intergalactic and
devouring evil.

They'll find allies: A wheelchair gunslinger from far-future
Beijing. A legion of women soldiers wielding Spinning
Saws that can slice through predators that only barely exist
inside our universe. A strange child-empath who can hear
all of humanity's suffering at every instant in history. A
firestarter-goddess from our prehistory. Together, they will
face a species that travels across time and feeds on terror
itself.

https://www.amazon.com/dp/1732086982
https://stantlitore.itch.io/ansible-omnibus

STANT LITORE

—NYOTA'S—
TYRANNOSAUR

Nyota's Tyrannosaur

Meet Nyota Madaki and her tyrannosaur. Fighting for survival in the far future.

Stranded inside the world where massive dinosaurs are grown for the arenas, Nyota will face many perils—the hunger of nocturnal predators, the crash of starvation, and the devouring rot of a bioweapon unleashed inside the tyrannosaur world while war in space rages just outside.

But Nyota is ready. Inhabited by entire ecosystems of nanites, trained for strength and speed and elegance, capable of feats that would leave others broken on the forest floor, Nyota can handle anything. Anything, that is, except the sudden rush of forgotten memories into her heart. Anything but the realization of who she really is.

Luckily she won't have to face that alone. Not with this tyrannosaur egg hatching beside her.

https://www.amazon.com/dp/B07FQ76J2Q

"Stant Litore turns a concept that would be clunky, camp, or just plain weird in other hands into something as natural as feeling the stretch of your own muscles when you move." —O.E. Tearmann, author of The Hands We're Given *(Aces High, Jokers Wild)*

LIVES OF
UNFORGETTING
WHAT WE LOSE IN TRANSLATION WHEN WE READ THE BIBLE

STANT LITORE

LIVES OF UNFORGETTING

THE ANCIENT GREEK WORD FOR "TRUTH" MEANS *unconcealing* or *unforgetting.* Yet today many ideas and stories that were once critical to how early Christians understood and practiced their faith often remain "hidden in plain sight" in our Bibles. These ideas are concealed from us by the distance between languages, eras, and cultures—yet they are so worth unconcealing and unforgetting. In this book, discover:

- The forgotten women who co-founded Christianity
- Whether the early church thought there was a hell
- What happens when you realize that in Greek, faith is a verb
- Why gender in the Bible is more complicated than we think
- Which concepts our modern tradition takes for granted that would have been alien to the original readers (like homophobia)

We have also forgotten that to read the Bible is to receive an invitation to adventure—to encounter the impossible, to move mountains, to walk on water. Instead, we have been taught to read the Bible tamely, to make no choices, to risk no questioning of our tradition. What would happen if we stepped out of the boat of our received tradition, out onto the crashing waves?

https://www.amazon.com/dp/1732086931